THIS BOOK BELONGS TO

NAME: _____

TO MY DAUGHTER RAEGAN.

AS I WATCH YOU GROW I SEE MYSELF.
THIS CHARACTER SKYLAR REPRESENTS YOU AND I.
REMEMBER YOU ARE PRECIOUS,
YOU ARE LOVED.

HI. MY NAME IS SKYLAR. THERE IS SOMETHING
SPECIAL ABOUT ME THAT I'D LIKE TO
SHARE WITH YOU.
I AM ADOPTED

I HAVE A LARGE BLENDED FAMILY THAT I LOVE SO MUCH! I HAVE MY BIOLOGICAL FAMILY AND I HAVE MY ADOPTED FAMILY.

SOME LIVE UP THE STREET ...
BUT SOME LIVE FAR AWAY.

SOME LOOK LIKE ME ... AND SOME DO NOT.

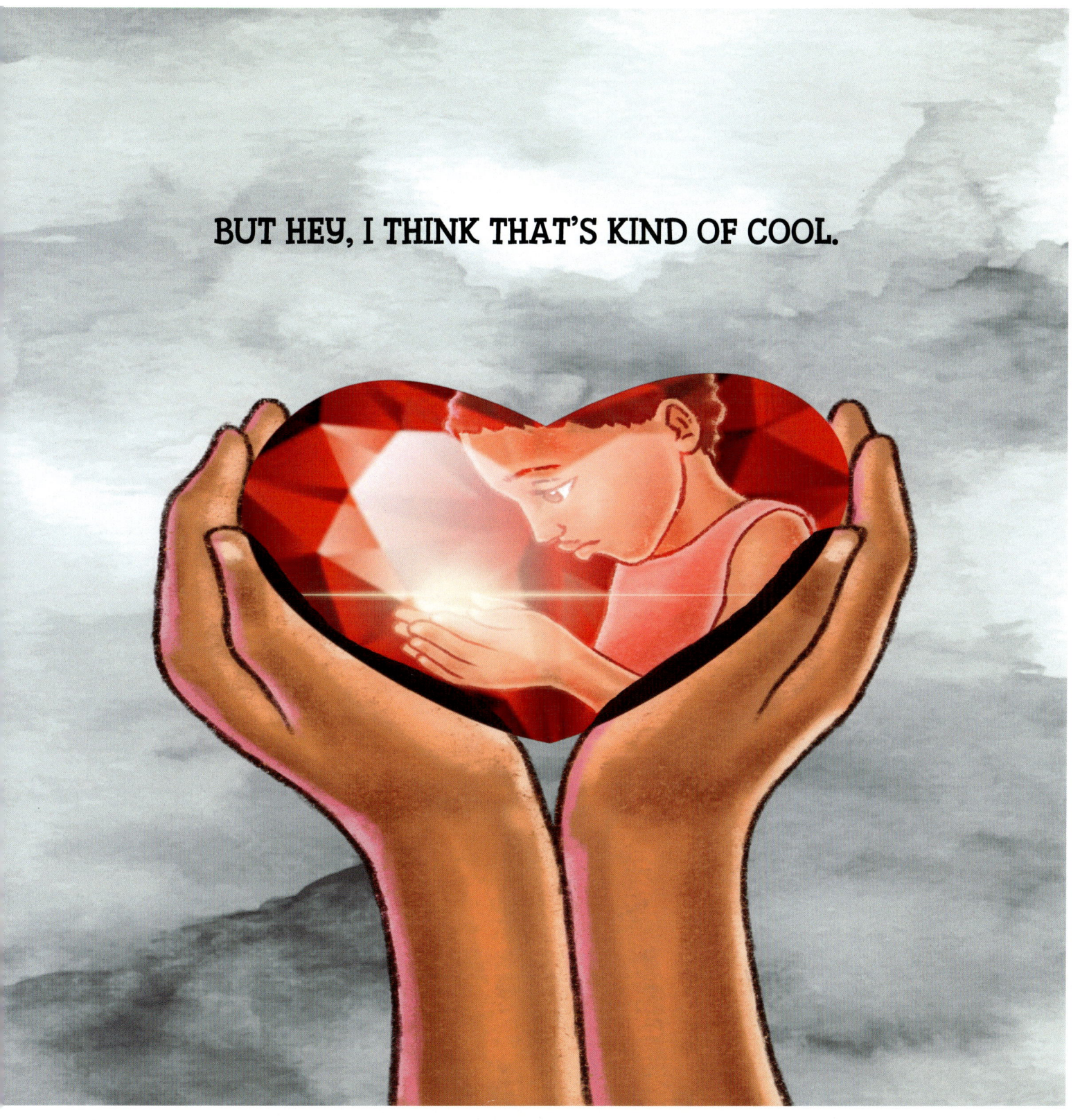

SUCH A LARGE FAMILY MEANS A LOT OF LOVE!
I SHOULD BE HAPPY, RIGHT?

WAS I NOT WANTED? ... WAS I A BAD GIRL? ...
DID I DO SOMETHING WRONG?

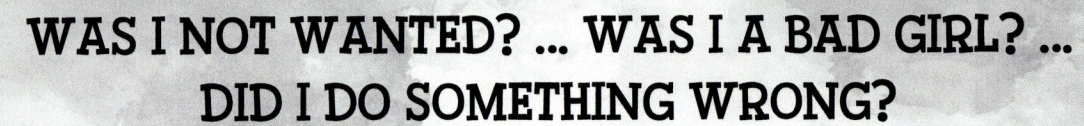

NO! I AM PRECIOUS, AND I AM LOVED! MY BIOLOGICAL FAMILY LOVES ME AND ALWAYS WILL. I AM A SPECIAL CHILD WHO WAS GIVEN A CHANCE TO BE LOVED BY A NEW FAMILY.

BUT SOMETIMES I FEEL

ANGRY

LONELY

GUILTY

SAD

LOST

CURIOUS

AFRAID

IT IS OKAY TO FEEL DIFFERENT EMOTIONS.
BEING ADOPTED IS SOMETHING EXTRA SPECIAL,
IN FACT.

THAT MAKES MY FAMILY LOVE ME EVEN MORE,
BECAUSE I AM PRECIOUS, AND I AM LOVED.

I KNOW THIS BECAUSE EVERY DAY I AM REMINDED
BY MY FAMILY. ESPECIALLY WHEN ...

I GET EXTRA CUDDLES FROM MOMMY AND DADDY.

WHEN I GET TO BAKE YUMMY COOKIES
WITH MOMMY.

WHEN I GET TO GO FISHING WITH DADDY.

BUT MOST OF ALL, IT IS WHEN I HEAR THE WORDS
"I LOVE YOU."

YOU ARE PRECIOUS
YOU ARE LOVED

"TO BE ADOPTED MEANS YOU ARE SPECIAL. IT MEANS YOU ARE PRECIOUS, YOU ARE LOVED. WHAT AN AMAZING GIFT YOU HAVE BECOME TO YOUR NEW FAMILY. NOTHING CAN REPLACE THAT SPECIAL PLACE IN YOUR BIOLOGICAL OR YOUR ADOPTIVE FAMILIES' HEARTS. YOU WILL HAVE ENDLESS LOVE AND SUPPORT, SO NEVER FORGET THAT ...
I AM PRECIOUS,
I AM LOVED."

WHAT MAKES YOU HAPPY?

DRAW YOUR FAMILY